The Pirate Who Couldn't Name Her Ship

by Sara Sutton

DORRANCE
PUBLISHING CO
EST. 1920
PITTSBURGH, PENNSYLVANIA 15238

Dorrance Publishing Co
585 Alpha Drive
Suite 103
Pittsburgh, PA 15238
Visit our website at *www.dorrancebookstore.com*

ISBN: 978-1-4809-1870-2
eISBN: 978-1-4809-1847-4

To all of the little pirate kids

May the wind always find your sails

The seas were roaring.
The sun was high.
The horizon stretched miles wide.

Jane was hollering, "Man the sails!"
Every crew member
from Peg-Legged Jim to One-Eyed Jack
followed her every command.

When up in the crow's nest
Came a shout to below.
"Captain Jane!
A problem I have come to know!"

Gold–Toothed Gus skittered on down.
Captain Jane eyed him
with a worried frown.
"What could possibly be wrong?"
Jane wondered aloud.
"The crew is well, the ship is sturdy,
the wind is abiding, and we are in a hurry…"

Gus nodded along until she was done.
"We have followed the   map day and night…
The buried treasure is   so close I can taste…
But something just   isn't right…

Your beautiful ship doesn't have a name!"

Jane stood in shock, "By gosh you are right! Oh just let me think... I'll come up with something by night!"
But of course a good captain wants help from her crew....
"Who can be the first to come up with something bold, brilliant, and new?"

So, the crew had a meeting down in the kitchen,
But none of the pirates could make a decision.
Polly the parrot suggested, Feathered Friend...
And Moody Molly vouched for The Rage of Seaweed.
None of these names just seemed to sum up,
What the ship meant to each and every one.

Oh, how those
pirates racked their brains,

But none struggled as much as Captain Jane.
She twirled her curls and bit her nails,
Wondering how she could miss
Such an important detail

Down in her cabin Jane jotted list after list
But every name was a hit and miss
"Well it's very cozy and warm...
And shows no fear when the seas begins to storm.

The deck is always shiny, polished so clean
And the fish give the bottom kisses
so it's not algae green."

Then she tried to think
of her favorite things,
Puppies, purple, and shiny gold,
Decorative hats new and old...
Slash after slash she marked things off.
Her mood grew further irate and
Somewhat cross.

"The Jolly Roger
is taken by Captain Hook
And Redbeard has his mark
on nearly everything in the book."
So what does that leave for Captain Jane?
She needs something original
to stake her claim.

Soft and quiet
she muttered to herself
So her crew wouldn't hear and fall into distress,
"C'mon Jane get a grip,
Or you'll be the only pirate
who couldn't name her ship."

When a crack of thunder
sounded from above,
And the choppy waves
that a pirate loves
Rocked the ship this way and that
Made a mess of the den
and her collection of hats.

Jane's quick feet carried
her out onto deck,
But the gray clouds and lightning
were one step ahead.

Orders ran off
the Captain's lips,
And she feared what this storm
would make of her ship,
But she soon rest assured
because by looking around,
A hard working crew
is exactly what she found.

They ignored the slippery rain,
And the flood of the waves

Sailing right on to the end of the storm,
And when they made it Gus gladly informed,
"Ah, no worries Cap'n, clear skies ahead."

Molly grabbed the mop,
"I'll take care of this mess!"

And just when Jane wondered
if they had been blown off track,
Jim showed her that they've
remained true to the map

Jane felt at ease and so proud,
Because she had realized what her ship is all about,
Adventures, high waves, and friends gathered 'round.

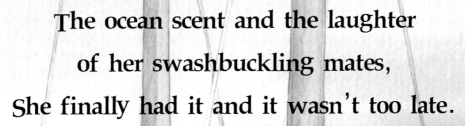

The ocean scent and the laughter
of her swashbuckling mates,
She finally had it and it wasn't too late.

The sun had just fallen
and the moon was on the rise,
And her fellow sailors knew
that she had made up her mind.

That night they all slept well with giddy smiles,

Pride

Because they were floating on Salty Pride.